BRIGHT IDEA BOOKS

MISTY Copeland

by Golriz Golkar

CAPSTONE PRESS
a capstone imprint

Bright Idea Books are published by Capstone Press
1710 Roe Crest Drive, North Mankato, Minnesota 56003
www.mycapstone.com

Copyright © 2019 by Capstone Press, a Capstone imprint. All rights reserved. No part of this publication may be reproduced in whole or in part, or stored in a retrieval system, or transmitted in any form or by any means, electronic, mechanical, photocopying, recording, or otherwise, without written permission of the publisher.

Library of Congress Cataloging-in-Publication Data
Names: Golkar, Golriz, author.
Title: Misty Copeland / by Golriz Golkar.
Description: North Mankato, Minnesota : Capstone Press, [2019] | Series: Influential people | Summary: «Learn about how Misty Copeland broke barriers for dancers of color and worked her way to the top»-- Provided by publisher. | Includes bibliographical references and index.
Identifiers: LCCN 2018019505 (print) | LCCN 2018025897 (ebook) | ISBN 9781543541700 (ebook) | ISBN 9781543541304 (hardcover : alk. paper)
Subjects: LCSH: Copeland, Misty--Juvenile literature. | Ballet dancers--United States--Biography--Juvenile literature. | African American women dancers--Biography--Juvenile literature. | LCGFT: Biographies.
Classification: LCC GV1785.C635 (ebook) | LCC GV1785.C635 G65 2019 (print) | DDC 792.8092 [B] --dc23
LC record available at https://lccn.loc.gov/2018019505

Editorial Credits
Editor: Mirella Miller
Designer: Becky Daum
Production Specialist: Megan Ellis

Quote Source
p. 27, "6 Misty Copeland Quotes That Will Inspire You To Break Through Barriers Too." *Bustle*, July 1, 2015

Photo Credits
AP Images: Bebeto Matthews, 14, Desmond Boylan, 12–13, Diane Bondareff/Invision, 26–27, Evan Agostini/Invision, cover; Newscom: Dennis Van Tine/ZUMA Press, 8–9, Ricky Fitchett/ZUMA Press, 5, 24, Ruslan Shamukov/ZUMA Press, 21; Rex Features: Cindy Barrymore, 18–19, David Buchan/Variety, 6–7; Shutterstock Images: lev radin, 17, 23, 31; YearbookLibrary: Seth Poppel, 11

Design Elements: iStockphoto, Red Line Editorial, and Shutterstock Images

TABLE OF CONTENTS

CHAPTER ONE
A STAR BALLERINA 4

CHAPTER TWO
AN UNLIKELY START 10

CHAPTER THREE
DANCING TO THE TOP 16

CHAPTER FOUR
BEYOND BALLET 22

Glossary 28
Timeline 29
Activity 30
Further Resources 32
Index 32

CHAPTER 1

A STAR Ballerina

The drums rolled. The ballerina spun. She took a final leap. She folded her swan wings. The lights lowered. The dancer disappeared into the darkness.

The audience cheered. The dancers took a bow. It was a great performance of *Swan Lake*. Everyone clapped for Misty Copeland, the star. Copeland smiled and bowed.

Copeland took a bow after finishing a performance in 2015.

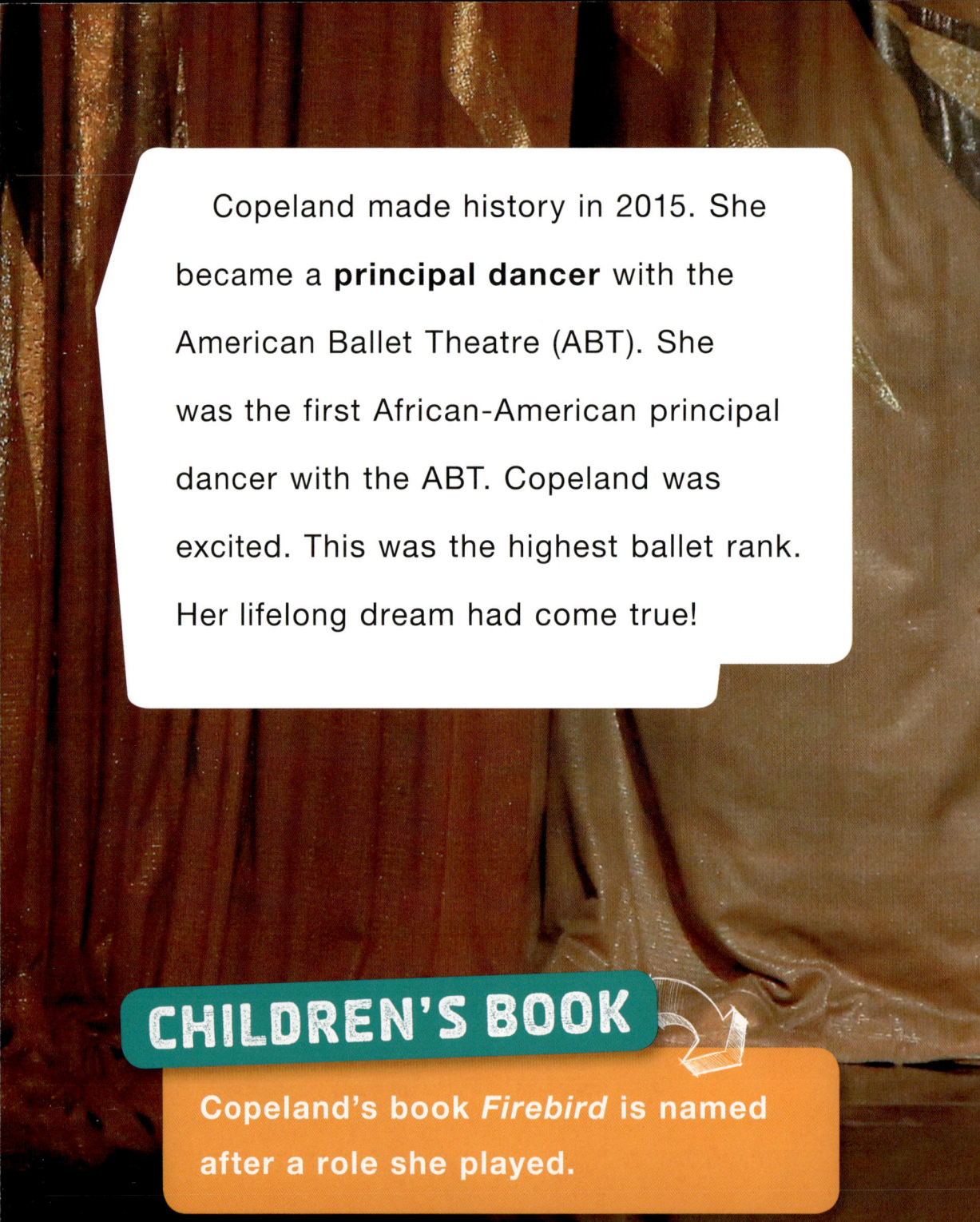

Copeland made history in 2015. She became a **principal dancer** with the American Ballet Theatre (ABT). She was the first African-American principal dancer with the ABT. Copeland was excited. This was the highest ballet rank. Her lifelong dream had come true!

CHILDREN'S BOOK

Copeland's book *Firebird* is named after a role she played.

Copeland trained hard to become the dancer she is today.

Copeland stayed focused on her dreams.

It had been a tough road. People said she was too short and muscular. Some said Copeland joined ballet too late. But she refused to let go of her dreams.

CHAPTER 2

AN UNLIKELY Start

Misty Copeland was born in Missouri. Her family was poor. They moved often. They finally settled in California.

Copeland enjoyed dancing at home. But she had no **formal** dance experience. Copeland wanted to try out for her school's drill team when she was 13 years old. They danced at school events.

Copeland started dancing later in her childhood.

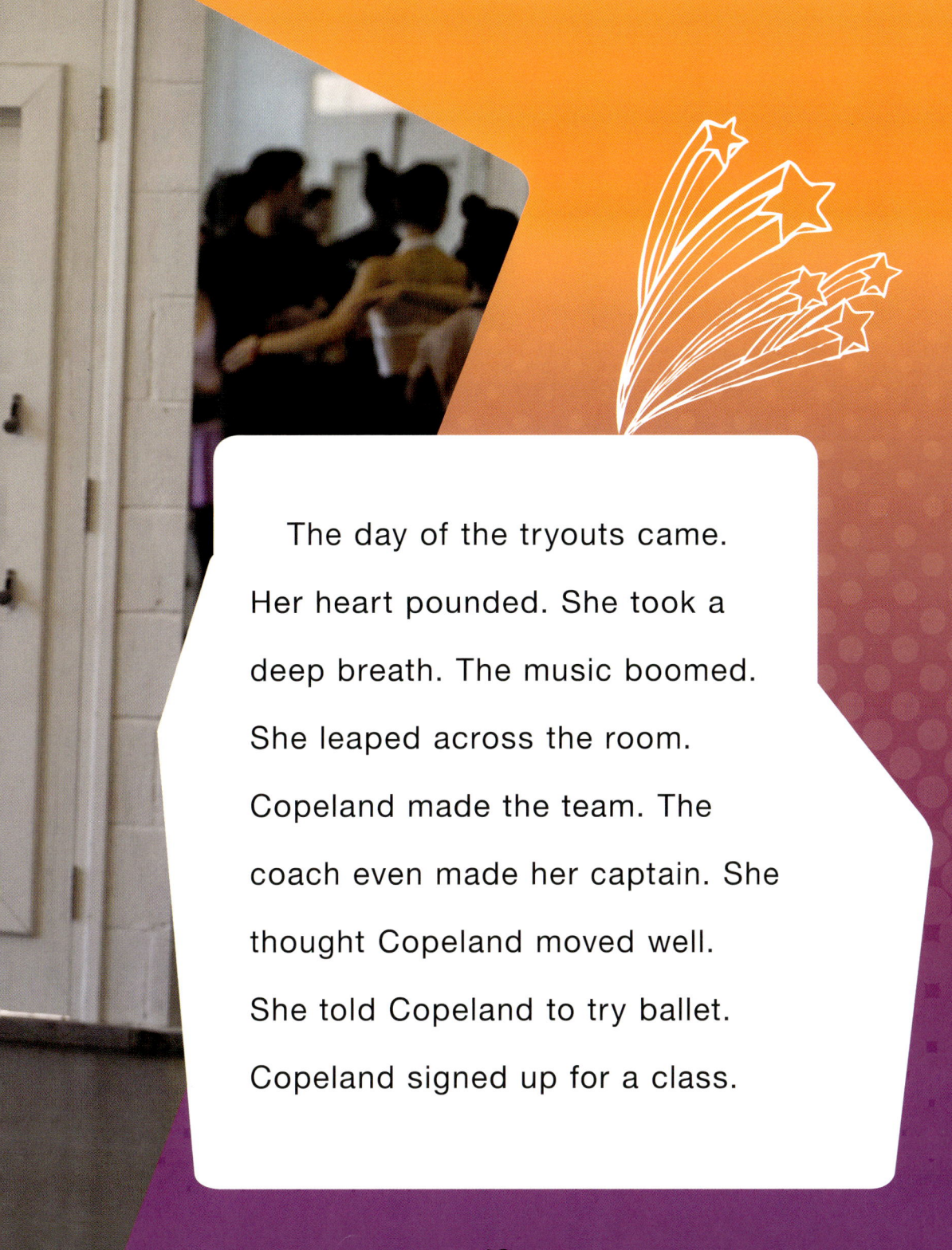

The day of the tryouts came. Her heart pounded. She took a deep breath. The music boomed. She leaped across the room. Copeland made the team. The coach even made her captain. She thought Copeland moved well. She told Copeland to try ballet. Copeland signed up for a class.

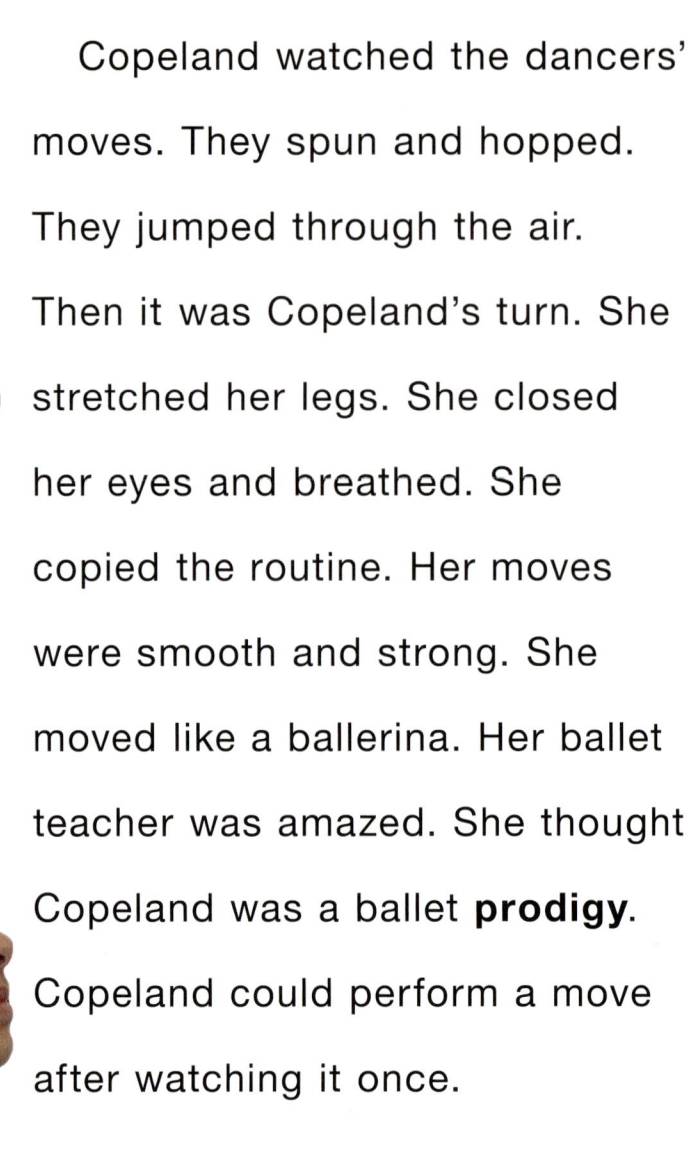

Copeland watched the dancers' moves. They spun and hopped. They jumped through the air. Then it was Copeland's turn. She stretched her legs. She closed her eyes and breathed. She copied the routine. Her moves were smooth and strong. She moved like a ballerina. Her ballet teacher was amazed. She thought Copeland was a ballet **prodigy**. Copeland could perform a move after watching it once.

Copeland took as many classes as possible to perfect her skills.

Copeland took more classes. She learned quickly. She started dancing on **pointe**. Professional dancers dance on pointe.

Copeland's dream was to dance for the ABT. She kept practicing. She would try out for the ABT one day.

FAST LEARNER

Most ballet dancers take three years to dance on pointe. Copeland took eight weeks!

CHAPTER 3

DANCING to the Top

Copeland earned a summer **scholarship** to the ABT at age 18. Copeland danced well. The ABT invited her to join the company. She would be a professional ballerina. She would perform in big shows. Copeland's hard work had paid off.

Copeland became a role model for many young dancers.

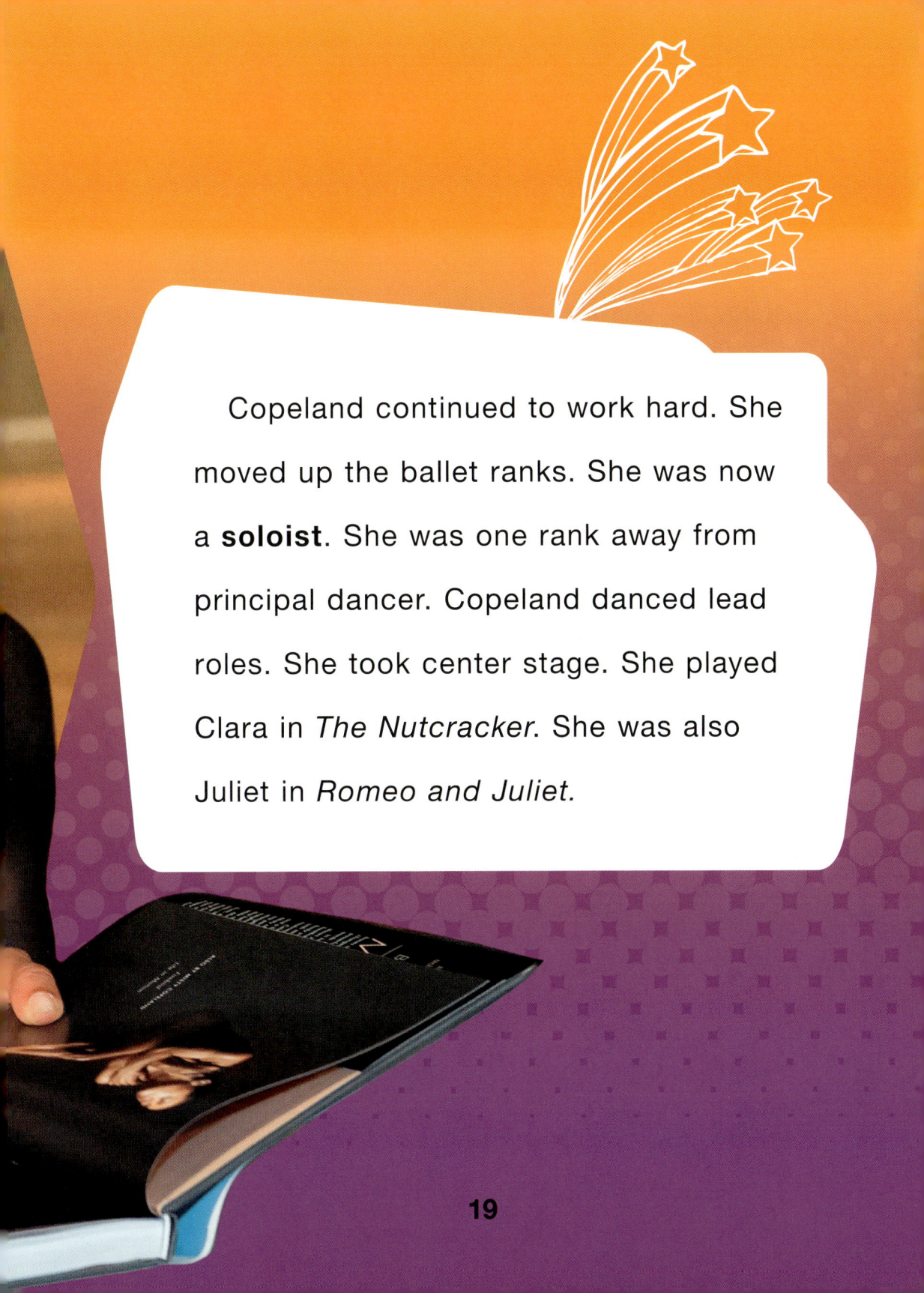

Copeland continued to work hard. She moved up the ballet ranks. She was now a **soloist**. She was one rank away from principal dancer. Copeland danced lead roles. She took center stage. She played Clara in *The Nutcracker*. She was also Juliet in *Romeo and Juliet.*

She amazed people with her moves. She was elegant and strong. Other dancers were watching her. They followed her lead.

OVERCOMING OBSTACLES

Copeland was reaching her dream. But she still had trouble. People talked about her **race**. There were few African Americans in ballet. She felt alone.

Copeland did not have a typical dancer's body. Some people said she was too heavy. She also had many injuries. But each time, she bounced back. Copeland never gave up!

Copeland posed during a ballet practice.

CHAPTER 4

BEYOND
Ballet

Copeland has been successful outside ballet. She danced in a **Broadway** musical in 2015. She had a lead role. Copeland's energy lit up the stage.

Copeland spends time helping young people. She is a **mentor**. She coaches young dancers to reach their dreams. Her work with children has been honored.

Copeland smiled after her Broadway debut.

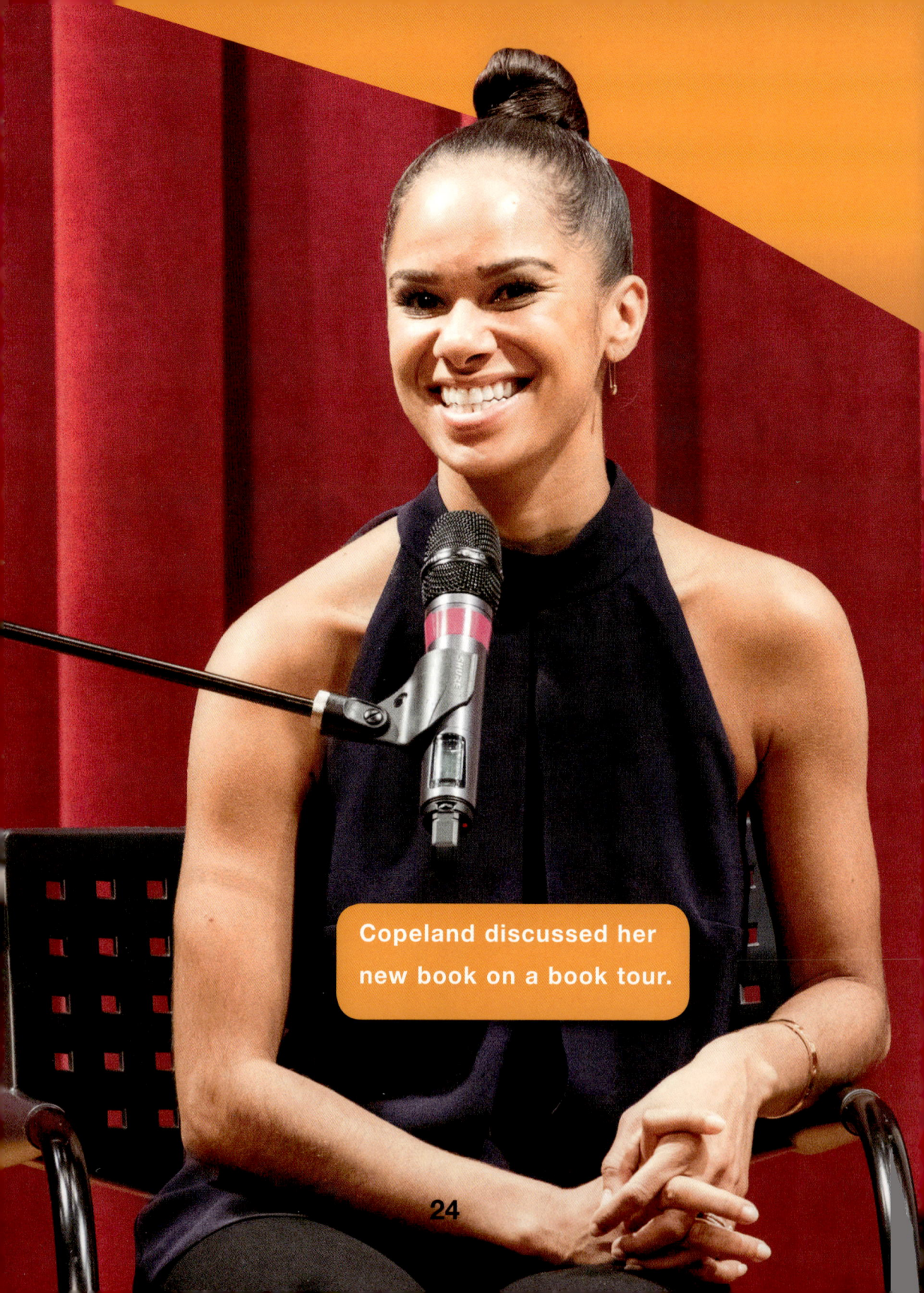

Copeland discussed her new book on a book tour.

In 2015, Copeland starred in a movie about her life. It was called *A Ballerina's Tale*. Copeland has written a best-selling **memoir**. *Life in Motion* is the name of the book. She also wrote a children's book titled *Firebird*.

Copeland posed with the Barbie doll created for her.

BARBIE DOLL

Copeland has a Barbie doll named after her.

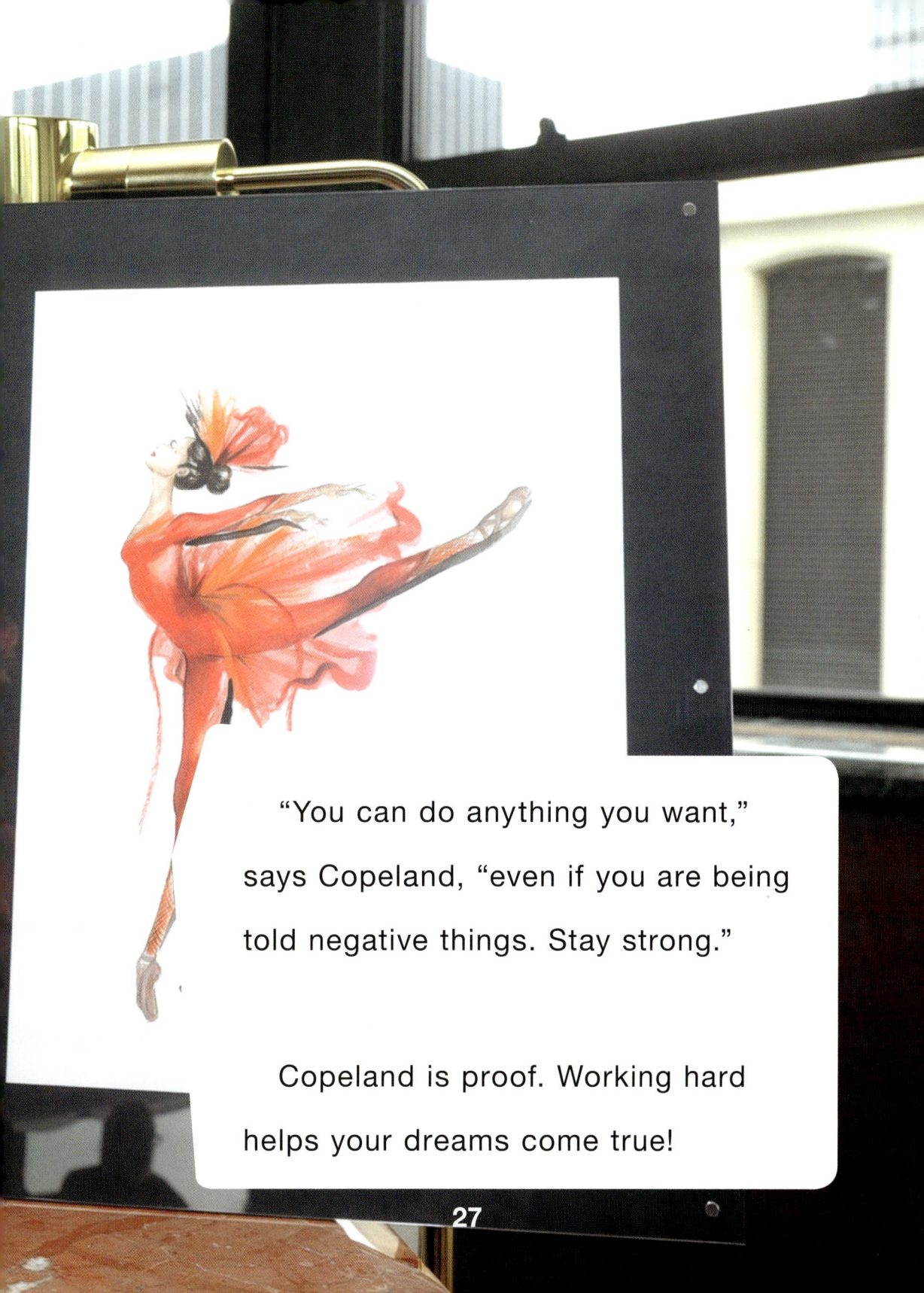

"You can do anything you want," says Copeland, "even if you are being told negative things. Stay strong."

Copeland is proof. Working hard helps your dreams come true!

GLOSSARY

Broadway
a theater district in New York City where many famous shows are performed

formal
official; marked by form or ceremony

memoir
a book about someone's life, written by that person

mentor
someone who acts as a teacher or guide for another person

pointe
a French ballet term meaning "on the tips of the toes"

principal dancer
the highest rank in professional ballet

prodigy
a young person with genius-level abilities

race
a group of people sharing common physical characteristics passed down through generations

scholarship
money given to a student to help pay for education, sometimes earned through high grades or achievements

soloist
a ballet dancer who is one rank above the group dancers and one rank below a principal dancer

TIMELINE

1982: Misty Copeland is born.

1998: Copeland earns a full scholarship to the San Francisco Ballet summer program.

2001: Copeland joins the American Ballet Theatre's (ABT) corps de ballet, their main company.

2007: The ABT promotes Copeland to soloist.

2012: Copeland performs one of her most famous roles in *Firebird*.

2014: President Barack Obama chooses Copeland for the President's Council on Fitness, Sports, and Nutrition.

2015: Copeland becomes the first African American female principal dancer at the ABT.

ACTIVITY

INTERVIEW AN INSPIRING PERSON!

Misty Copeland is an inspiring person. She worked very hard to make her dreams come true. Her life has not always been easy, but she never gave up!

Think of a person who inspires you. How do you know this person? What is this person's job or role in your life? Why does he or she inspire you? Has he or she had challenges in life? Write some questions you would like to ask this person, and interview him or her. Maybe this person can offer advice on making dreams come true!

FURTHER RESOURCES

Love learning about Misty Copeland? Learn more in these books:

Copeland, Misty. *Firebird*. New York: G. P. Putnam's Sons Books for Young Readers, 2014.

Copeland, Misty. *Life in Motion: An Unlikely Ballerina*. New York: Aladdin Young Readers, 2016.

Ryals, Lexi. *When I Grow Up: Misty Copeland*. New York: Scholastic, 2016.

How is Copeland changing ballet and changing lives? Learn more here:

How to Win at Life: Tips from Ballerina Misty Copeland
https://www.teenvogue.com/story/misty-copeland-interview-92nd-street-y

Misty Copeland Is Changing the Way We Think About Ballet Dancers
https://www.sikids.com/si-kids/2016/06/29/misty-copeland-changing-way-we-think-about-ballet-dancers

INDEX

American Ballet Theatre (ABT), 6, 15, 16

Ballerina's Tale, A, 25
Barbie, 26
Broadway, 22

Copeland, Misty
ballet classes, 13–15
drill team, 11
family, 10
injuries, 20
mentor, 23
scholarship, 16

Firebird, 6, 25

Life in Motion, 25

Nutcracker, 19

pointe, 15

Romeo and Juliet, 19

Swan Lake, 5